Tweet Sarts

Tweet Sarts

An Anderson Family Chronicle

This book is a work of fiction.
Any reference to historical events, real people,
or real locales is used fictitiously.
Other names, characters, places and incidents
are the product of the author's imagination,
and any resemblance to actual events, locales
or persons, living or dead, is entirely
coincidental.

ISBN-13: 978-1519583673
ISBN-10: 1519583672

Chapter One

Hector Anderson waded through rubble in the destroyed street. Cars, strewn about like matchbox toys, burned. Thick, acrid smoke stung his eyes and made breathing almost impossible. Air alert sirens wailed. He pulled off his glasses and wiped grime from the lenses. It seemed so unreal. He shook his head, trying to dislodge his memory

KaBLAU!

Metal shards pinned down his legs and rained on his soft pillow.

Soft pillow? None of this made any sense.

He woke to find that the space ship drone was really his alarm clock. The air alert siren was Mom's teakettle whistling in the kitchen. No metal shards pinned down his legs, just a tangled mess of sheets.

He felt himself slipping back into his dream. A familiar voice spoke behind him. In his confusion, he couldn't place it.

"Get up, Hec," it said.

He crunched his body down, hiding as best he could behind the charred wreck.

"I said get up."

He opened his eyes and encountered the most frightening alien he'd ever seen. It had corpse-pale skin and a great, bulbous green brain protruding from the top of its head. It opened purple-black lips and leaned close.

"Aargh! Leave me alone!" he screamed, flailing his arms.

"Jeez, what's your problem? You're going to miss breakfast."

Breakfast? He fumbled on the nightstand for his glasses, crammed them on his face, and realized that this was no freak from outer space. This was his sister Chloe, the high school gothic drama freak. Chloe rewrapped the green towel around her hair, gave a snort of impatience, and stomped out of the room.

Hec groaned. A weird dream like that was almost enough to make him swear off eating an entire large pepperoni pizza while watching alien invader movies. He pulled on his jeans, with yesterday's underwear still in them, threw on a rumpled flannel shirt, socks and sneakers, ran a hand through his tangled curls, and ambled down for breakfast.

Mr. Buttons, his brother Calvin's puppet, waved at Hec as he entered the kitchen. Calvin, the smartest fourth grader in the universe, didn't seem to notice what his left hand was doing. He and Stevie, Hec's baby brother, hunched over stacks of steaming pancakes, shoveling them in as if they hadn't eaten in a week. Behind them was a wall of newspaper and behind that, Hec assumed, was Dad. Mom, in her old fuzzy pink robe, flipped pancakes at the stove.

"Morning, honey bunny," she said. "Is your sister up?"

"Ooom. This is good," he said. He didn't sound that different from Stevie when his mouth was stuffed.

"Special pancakes for a special day," Mom said.

Dad's newspaper wall crashed down. He looked at his watch and jumped from his chair. "I'll say it's special," he said. "There's a test today on the range. Top Secret. Gotta get going. I need extra time to go through clearance." He gave Mom a quick peck on the cheek and rushed out the door, his napkin still tucked into the collar of his shirt.

"What was that all about?" Chloe said as she walked into the kitchen. Chloe's pale makeup and dark eyeliner made her look like a ghoul. Her dark lipstick matched her Kool-Aid purple hair. As always, she wore a black sweater and black jeans.

"Daddy's preoccupied with a field test. He forgot what day it is," Mom said with a sigh.

"Monday?" asked Hec. Dad was always preoccupied and absent-minded. Scientists were like that. Rocket scientists, like Hec's dad, were the worst.

"Monday, yes. And the day of a big test on the range. It's also our anniversary. How could he lose track of a special day like that?" Mom asked.

"I don't wose twack of special days! It's a hunnert and twennyfree days till my birfday!" Stevie waved a forkful of sticky pancakes for emphasis.

"And four before you go to the dentist," Mom said with a laugh. As if that was special.

4

Chloe rolled her eyes as she dropped into her seat. She studied a pancake, and then settled for orange juice. "Celebrating anniversaries is so bourgeois. It's a scam run by the greeting card, florist, and candy conglomerates."

"Chloe Marie Anderson! Surely you don't believe that," Mom said. "Cards and flowers and candy make people feel special."

Chloe snorted. "External sources do nothing for true self-esteem. Besides, don't you think you're too old for silly things like that?"

Mom's hands flew to her face. "I don't look old, do I?" she gasped.

"Of course you do! You're our mother!" Mr. Buttons squeaked from atop Calvin's hand. The boy and the puppet looked at each other and nodded. Calvin's gold-rimmed glasses and Mr. Button's paper clip ones bobbed in unison.

Hec could tell by the look on Mom's face that now would be a good time to go. He gave Mom a sticky ___ ___ ___. "Maybe Dad's saving his surp___ ___ ___ ta go. Eddie's waiting on the ___ ___ ___ ___ his stuff and escaped into th___ ___ ___ ___.

Chapter Two

"I hate Mondays," Hec said as he and Eddie Hernandez trudged toward Desert Ridge Middle School.

"I hate 'em worse," Eddie answered. The words seemed as sharp as the ends of Eddie's hair, which he'd recently taken to spiking straight up. Hec thought it made him look like Sonic the hedgehog, but he was too polite to tell his friend that.

we're not getting anywhere

said sullenly.

with his hands deep in his pockets, his shoulders slumped so far forward they nearly met in front. His bottom lip stuck out enough to be a landing pad for birds. Hec wasn't used to having to comfort Eddie.

"What's the problem?" Hec asked.

"What's your problem?" Eddie snapped back.

This comforting stuff wasn't going to be easy.

"My mom. She's acting real weird this morning," Hec said, hoping his admission would help Eddie open up.

"At least she's around to act weird," said Eddie.

"Your mom working a lot?"

"Worse. Gone."

Hec stopped walking. "Whad'ja mean, gone?"

"Gone. My mom and dad had a fight. She packed a suitcase and went to live with Tia Maria in the North Valley."

The words hit Hec harder than any bad test grade ever had. His stomach went sour. No wonder Eddie was in such a bad mood. How would he feel if his mom left? "Whoa," Hec said, searching for the right words. There didn't seem to be any. "I'm like, sorry, Eddie. Real sorry."

"Don't be sorry for me," Eddie said a little too defensively. He wiped his eyes with the back of his hand and started walking so fast that Hec had to jog to catch up. "I'm not going to let it change my life. Who cares that Mom's gone? It's not like she was around much to begin with. It's not like I had some great family life anyway with both of 'em working all the time. Things aren't going to change for me one bit. Ya goin' to the dance?"

Eddie's bombshell about his Mom had startled Hec so much that he had trouble thinking about anything else. "What dance?"

"Man, Hec! Where have you been? Outer space? The Valentine's Day dance after school on Friday. Remember?"

"Oh, yeah. That dance." School was in sight and Hec didn't have much time to recover. "Nothing ever happens at those dances."

"I'd go for the cookies," Eddie recommended. "Those PTA moms make really good cookies."

The bell rang just as they entered the door. Hec dug through his backpack for a pencil as he struggled upstream to math class while Eddie waded toward the gym.

Silly Eddie, Hec thought with a chuckle. *He has a fit, he doesn't have to brush his hair or take a shower before school, yet he does anyway. And now Eddie was spending hours getting his hair to spike. Eddie was almost as silly as me when it came to spending time on hair. If he had PE first, he wouldn't bother with stuff like that. Not that he did, anyway. He saved* pincushion of a hairdo when he walked into class and stopped dead.

WHOOP! WHOOP! WHOOP!

Warning sirens screamed in Hec's brain. His jaw dropped and the pencil clattered to the floor in front of the most beautiful girl in the universe. Before he could do anything, she scooped it up and held it out to him.

"You dropped your pencil," she said, flashing a dimpled smile. She had the bluest, sparkliest eyes Hec had ever seen.

"Uh," said Hec. His hands remained frozen on his backpack.

"I'm Sandy Richardson," she said, slipping the pencil into the pocket of his flannel shirt. "I just moved here. From Topeka."

"Uh," Hec said.

Mr. Grumbolt clapped his hands to get everyone's attention. "Okay, class. Let's get going. Sandy, take that empty seat between Hector and Paul." Hec lurched forward, but while his legs knew where he needed to go, his brain was still trying to make sense of Sandy. He crashed into his desk, spilling the contents of his backpack all over the floor.

"Smooth move, ExLax," whispered Wes Snyder, the center for Desert Ridge Middle School's basketball team, who sat behind Hec. "Way to impress the new girl."

"Shut up, Wesley," Hec muttered. He glanced up at Sandy, who blushed and tucked a golden curl behind her ear before she turned her attention to the front of the room.

"While Hector picks up his stuff, the rest of you can get out your homework," Mr. Grumbolt said. Hec scrambled around on hands and knees. He could hear his classmates snickering. He'd never live this down. Never in a million, bazillion years. He'd have to move to a galaxy far, far away and be an outcast for the rest of his feeble existence. But he didn't mind. Sandy knew who he was.

Chapter Three

"There's a new girl in my math class," Hec said to Eddie on their way home from school.

"Must be Sandy," Eddie replied.

WHOOP! WHOOP! WHOOP!

The warning sirens in Hec's brain screamed again. Hec tried to act casual but he felt light headed and dizzy. "You know her?" Hec's voice cracked its way through three octaves as he asked.

"Yeah," Eddie answered. "She lives next door, in the Mueller's old place. Moved in this weekend. From Wichita or someplace."

"To bel—" Hec corrected. "I made a real fool out of myself right in front of her."

"So what else is new?" Eddie asked with a wink. He laughed back. Only Eddie could say something like that and make it not sound mean.

"Tell m—

fault my Mom left. Mom was making welcome-to- the- neighborhood-enchiladas and Dad made some crack about how it wasn't nice to poison them their very first day in the neighborhood. It was a joke, but Mom didn't think it was funny. Women!"

Eddie gave Hec's arm a friendly punch. Hec returned it. They were almost to the turnoff to Hec's block. Hec gazed up the street, wishing he had alien X-ray vision and could see around the curve and all the way to Eddie's house. "When my folks started fighting I went next door and helped her move her stuff in. It's all girly stuff: silly white furniture and tons of teddy bears. And lots of different colored polka dots all over the curtains, the bedspread, and the pillows. Like M&Ms without the M's printed on them. Made me hungry just looking at them.

"Hmmm," mused Hec. "Eddie buddy, I've been thinking. You've been picking me up before school for as long as I can remember. I think it's my turn to return the favor."

Eddie snorted in disbelief. "You mean, walk all the way up to my house? Man, Hec! You barely have enough time to find both shoes every morning."

"Yeah, I mean all the way up you your house," Hec said in an exasperated tone.

"Don't you think that's a little out of your way? After all, I have to walk right by your street to get to school. You'll be going an extra two blocks," Eddie pointed out.

"Anything for a friend," Hec said.

"AND a friend's neighbor," said Eddie as they parted.

Hec looked back twice. Maybe he'd need to ride his bike to Eddie's a little later, to get help on his homework. Pity they didn't have any of the same classes. Maybe he should finish his homework quickly, and then ride up to Eddie's house to console his good buddy. What with his mom problem and all, Eddie might need company. Hec was still considering what excuse to use as he passed the Nelson's hedge.

"Psst," said the hedge.

Hec nearly jumped out of his sneakers. His heart raced.

"Act casual," the bush said in a high, squeaky voice. "It's me, Mr. Buttons. A little red pom-pom nose appeared, and then pulled quickly back. Two black button eyes glistened deep within the hedge. Where Mr. Buttons was, Calvin was also.

Hec sighed. "Calvin, what in the world are you doing? This isn't another of your Calvin: Master Spy of the Universe ideas, is it?"

"Shh," the puppet answered. "She'll hear." Mr. Buttons jerked his head toward the Anderson house, where a little girl stood on the front step talking with someone inside the open door. The little girl had round glasses atop round, pink cheeks.

had to shake her. Don't tell her where I am, please?"

"I'm with ya, buddy," Hec said. He straightened his pack and, whistling casually, continued home.

Mom looked up as Hec approached. She frowned as he crossed the lawn and jumped the shrubs instead of coming up the walk, but she couldn't say anything – not with that girl as a witness.

Hec did a double take when he saw Mom. Fluorescent pink, green and blue rollers stuck out at odd angles all over head, making her look like some kind of weird-wired robot from outer space.

"Hec, honey, have you seen Calvin? I know he came home, but I can't find him. This is Callie. She's new in the neighborhood, and she's come over to play," Mom said. She cast a mildly worried look over Hec's shoulder.

"Haven't seen him," said Hec. It wasn't really a lie. All he'd seen in the murky depths of the hedge was Mr. Button's red pom-pom nose and the glimmer of button eyes. "But don't worry, Mom. I'm sure he's someplace close. What's for snack?"

"Peanut butter and graham crackers," Mom answered. "Callie, would you like to come in and have some while you wait?"

The little girl turned as pink as her jacket. "No, thank you, Mrs. Anderson. Mom said not to go into stranger's houses until she's met them. Besides, my sister's probably waiting for me."

WHOOP! WHOOP! WHOOP!

Hec's mental alarm went off again. New in the neighborhood! Sister! He looked closely at Callie. Blond hair. Blue eyes. Could it be? What had Eddie said Sandy's little sister's name was?

"Where'd you move from?" Hec asked. His voice cracked halfway through "you."

"Topeka."

Bingo! Hec felt his knees go weak. "Maybe I should walk you home. You being new in the neighborhood and all," Hec offered.

"Why Hec, how nice of you," said Mom.

Hec hoped Sandy would feel the same way. He dropped his backpack inside the front door and took off for Sandy's house, his heart pounding a million beats a minute.

"Do you know my sister? Her name's Sandy. She's in the seventh grade. She had lots of boyfriends back in Topeka. In Topeka she had to ride a bus and I walked. Now it's the other way around an' . . ." Callie babbled the entire way up her," he whispered. "Your next door neighbor's really an alien, sent to spy on us earthlings."

They reached the house. Hec looked up at the second story windows. One had polka dot curtains. Bingo! Sandy's room! Hec's knees felt weak. What would he say? What would he do?

Callie rummaged in her backpack for her key. "Darn. Can't find my key I know it's in here someplace oh well Sandy'll let me in," she said in one whoosh of words. She pressed the doorbell. Hec heard it play "She'll be Coming Round the Mountain." Yip! Yip! Yip! A little dog skittered across the tiles and thudded into the door. It pawed frantically on the inside, keeping up a steady barrage of barks.

"Coming!" he heard. Suddenly Hec saw spots. Would he pass out?

"Got lots of homework! See ya later," he shouted and bounded for the safety of the sidewalk.

"Who was that?" Hec heard Sandy ask as he sprinted down the street.

"That dangerous boy from Maple Street. Watch out for him. He's trouble," Mrs. McLarty answered. Encounter number two, disaster number two. Hec couldn't wait for encounter number three.

Chapter Four

"Psst," the Nelson's hedge said again, causing Hec to leap out of his sneakers for the second time that day.

"Oh Geez, Calvin! Talk about scaring a guy to death! I'd forgotten you were in there!" Hec took off his glasses and wiped them on the front of his shirt. "You can come out now. The coast is clear." Mr. Buttons stuck his

"Yuck," said Mr. Buttons. "All girls are yuck. And the nice ones are the yuckiest. You'll never find me playing with some yucky girl." Mr. Buttons pointed at Mom's fluorescent curlers with his pinkie hand while his thumb hand covered his mouth in horror. "Yoicks! Your head's been wired!"

"Shhh. She's picking up radio transmissions from Mars," Hec joked.

Mom just shrugged. "Men are from Mars, Women are from Venus. Maybe I'll pick up your father. She ushered the boys into the kitchen.

Stevie looked up from his cup. He had a milk mustache. Graham cracker crumbs mixed with his freckles all the way up to his eyebrows. "Weally? Is women weally fwum Venus? Do dey haf gween skins? It dat why dey wears all dat stuffs on der faces?"

Hec ruffled his brother's blond crew cut. "Maybe, sport. They certainly are different, wherever they're from."

"Especially Topeka," Mr. Buttons said.

The front door slammed and Chloe slinked into the kitchen. She took one look at Mom and rolled her eyes a full circle. "Oh, Mom," she groaned. "I can't believe you've succumbed to the pressures of chauvinistic society. Why sacrifice your looks all day long just to look good for a man?"

"Unlike some people who sacrifice their looks all day long for no apparent reason whatsoever," Hec said, flicking a strand of Chloe's Kool-aide purple hair.

"It's not 'a man' who's coming home, it's your father. And if I want to look good for him, that's my decision," Mom said between clenched teeth. The phone rang and Mom picked it up. She tried to put the receiver near her left ear, but a giant purple roller blocked her. She switched to the other side. No better. Finally she settled for holding the receiver five inches away.

"Hello? Hello?" she shouted into the distant receiver. "Oh hi, Geoff. Late? How late? Why? But I thought the test was supposed to be early this morning! I see. Of course it's not your fault. If you don't mind, I won't wait up for you." Mom set down the receiver with slow, firm deliberation. She pulled a few curlers from her hair and dropped them into a mixing bowl.

"Who was dat?" Stevie spluttered through his cracker.

"Daddy. The testing on the range he left so early for hasn't even begun. Something about wind turbulence. Th___ ___ ___ going to the mall." She dropped the last of the rollers into the bowl, and then marched upstairs.

"Rampant consumerism isn't the answer to your problems! You need a sense of identity separate from Dad's," Chloe called after her.

"Okay, I'll be identified as the woman who racked up the biggest charge card bill in history," Mom said when she came back down. She'd changed into a nicer outfit and her hair was combed. Hec caught a whiff of perfume as she breezed past. Why did she need new clothes? She looked wonderful. She smelled wonderful. Even if she was his mom. Hec remembered that when he was Stevie's age he'd decided when he was old enough to marry, he was going to marry Mom. Now the thought embarrassed him.

Hec left the house. He jumped on his bike and rode up to Eddie's house. The sky was brilliant blue, without a single cloud to mar it. It was warm enough for just a sweater, the kind of day that fools you into thinking that Spring is just around the bend when it's not. Albuquerque was like that: just when everyone packs away their winter coats and sweaters, one last snowstorm dumps and inch or two.

Hec's mind reeled with jumbled thoughts. Why did this love thing have to be so tricky? Like the weather, it fools you into thinking that everything is fine, and then

BAM!

Why had Eddie's Mom left just because Mr. Hernandez made a dumb comment? Could that happen to his family? Mom and Dad had been married forever. They had four kids. Would Mom start thinking Dad didn't love her just because he was busy at work? And how could Dad, after all these years, forget their anniversary? Wasn't an anniversary, like a birthday, so special you counted how many more days until the next one? Mom and Dad really loved each other, didn't they?

Hec slowed as he rolled around the corner. He waved at Old Lady McLarty, who shook her garden spade back at him. Right next door, Sandy was watering a flowerbed in her front yard. Panic made his heart beat double-time. What should he do? Should he wave? Should he ride right past as if he hadn't seen her? Maybe he should he turn around and avoid a scene entirely. Too late. Sandy looked up. She smiled and waved.

"Hi Hec," she said. "Where ya goin?"

"Eddie's house. We're working on a quantum physics project. Top Secret," Hec answered in the deepest, most confident voice he could muster. Quantum physics! He didn't even know what that meant, except that it sounded impressive. He'd added the top-secret bit because it always sounded so cool when Dad said it. He smiled back at Sandy.

Hec slammed into Eddie's

Sandy dropped her hose and ran to him. "Are you alright?" she asked. She leaned over him. Her head blocked the sun, making her curls look like they glowed. If he wasn't afraid he'd never breathe again, he might be enjoying this moment.

"What was that sound? Man, Hec, what are you doing to my mailbox?" Eddie stomped down his front walk and joined Sandy.

"Trying to destroy it, the vandal!" Old Lady McLarty shouted from two doors down. For an old lady, she sure had good hearing.

"Wasn't looking where I was going," Hec gasped painfully.

"He was telling me about the quantum physics problem you two are working on," Sandy said. The awe in her voice both pleased and unsettled Hec.

"Quantum what?" Eddie's face wrinkled up in confusion. Hec clutched Eddie's ankle like a drowning man does a piece of driftwood and squeezed with all his remaining strength. "Ohhhh. Thaaaaat quantum physics problem. Very difficult to explain. Very complex. It's about, uhm, quantums and stuff," Eddie covered.

Hec shakily got to his feet. "I feel better now," he said and offered a wan smile. He hobbled over and studied his fallen bike. No damage at all. The bike had rolled right under the mailbox when Hec had wrapped himself around it. He picked the bike up and wheeled it towards Eddie's front door.

"Man, Hec, you sure have a unique way to get a girl's attention," Eddie said with a chuckle when the door was closed behind them.

"Yeah? But it works. I bet Sandy will never forget me," Hec said. And it was no lie. She'd probably still be telling "stupid Hec" stories when she was living in the old folk's home. He needed to make a last impression on Sandy-- a good one. But how?

Chapter Five

Hec stumbled down the stairs, attracted by the smell of bacon and toast. "Hey, big guy. What's the count?" he asked, rubbing Stevie's velvety crewcut.

"A hunnert and twenty-two," Stevie answered.

"And three days until the dentist," someone in a zebra print robe and pink, fluff-covered slippers said.

"Comforting," Hec said, but he could see that, with his brother's help, he'd lost the argument. He surveyed the room. Chloe was lazily stirring her glass of apple juice while she read some strange newspaper she'd dragged home. Calvin and Stevie were shoveling in scrambled eggs and bacon. "Dad come home last night?"

"Not until really late," Mom said as she scooped eggs onto Hec's plate. "Chloe, honey, want some eggs?''

"Yuck," Chloe said. She stomped her way to the cupboard and rummaged around. After much banging and clattering she came up with a plastic bag filled with granola.

"Is this free range granola?" she asked. Free range? Hec thought that had something to do with chickens, not granola. He wondered if Chloe was making a joke. Mom must not have gotten it either.

"Of course it's not free," Mom answered. "It cost $1.49 a pound at the supermarket."

Ding Dong!

The doorbell rang. Stevie and Calvin exploded from the table, knocking down chairs and scattering silverware in a frenzied effort to beat each other to the door. Hec elbowed through the fighting brothers. He opened the door to a uniformed deliveryman holding a bouquet of pink roses. Hec counted them. A full dozen.

"Delivery for a Miss Chloe Anderson," the man read off his clipboard.

"Hey Chloe, it's for you," Hec shouted over his shoulder.

Chloe slunk down the hall. She didn't look at all pleased about being called away from her paper. Her expression changed entirely when she saw what the man held. Chloe's pale face flushed pink. A smile curled both corners of her pouty lips. She stopped slouching and threw back her shoulders. Hec thought she suddenly looked pretty. She signed the delivery slip and gushed a sweet *goodbye* and *have a nice day* to the man. Hec hadn't seen his sister act so nice in a very, very long time.

"Look!" Chloe said as she paraded back into the kitchen.

"Aren't you the one who said flowers were meaningless gestures of rampant commercialism?" Mom asked.

"I said no such thing! Mom, this is so sweet." With trembling hands she ripped open the little envelope. Hec peered over her shoulder. The card read 'from a secret admirer.' Chloe blushed deep rose. She shoved the card into the front pocket of her jeans.

"Hey, Mom," Hec said. "There's a Valentine's Day dance after school on Friday. You don't mind if I go, do you?"

"Why should I mind?" Mom asked.

poetry slams to dances. Aren't dances sexist or mindless or something?"

"Mom! Be open-minded. It's not fair to judge something unless you've actually tried it." Chloe clutched her vase to her and marched up to her room.

"Valentine's! Dances! Yuck!" Mr. Buttons wiped his thumb hand across his yarn mouth as if to wipe away the sickly sweet taste of love.

"I wikes Balentimes Day. I gets wots of tweet sarts and pollylops at school," Stevie said. Hec ruffled his little brother's hair. For a kid, he had his priorities figured out pretty well.

"Just wait 'til your dentist appointment," Mom said. "Then we'll see what you think about tweetsarts and pollylops."

On the way to school, Hec told Eddie all about his sister's reaction to the flowers. How could a surly goth like Chloe suddenly turn girly-sweet? It was a miracle, kind of like a caterpillar changing into a butterfly. And she didn't even know who sent them!

Eddie tapped his chin with his index finger. "Hmmm. This gives me an idea. If I send flowers to Mom and she thinks Dad sent them, will she come back?"

"Don't you think that's your dad's job?" Hec asked.

"But if he doesn't do it, maybe I should," Eddie said.

"I dunno," Hec said with a shrug. "Sounds like a good way to dig yourself in deep."

"Ah, what would you know? You're the one who tries to impress girls by impressing yourself onto mailboxes. Let's see . . ." Eddie tapped his forefinger against his front teeth as he made his plan. "I'll grab Dad's wallet while he's in the shower and use the charge card to order them over the phone. No one'll ever know. It's perfect." Eddie slugged Hec's arm. Hard. Hec rubbed it and wondered. Is this what girls really wanted?

Hec was so preoccupied in math class that he didn't even notice the spitballs Wes Snyder shot at him. He kept glancing sideways at Sandy and trying to read her mind. Would she react to flowers the way Chloe had? What color would she want? Red? Yellow? Pink? What color had Eddie said her room was? Polka dots. That didn't help. Sandy looked so pretty in her purple striped shirt. Maybe he should buy purple flowers. Were there purple flowers?

Hec spent social studies wondering how much roses cost. He wondered how much money he had in the Skippy jar on his dresser but admitted it probably wasn't very much. He wished he hadn't bought three new packs of game cards last week. Suddenly they didn't seem very important.

During English he wondered if different flowers might do just as well. Were daisies cheaper than roses? It was a pity it wasn't summer. Then he could just cut some of his mom's fl

By lunch Hec was too hungry to think about Sandy. He wolfed down his tray of mystery meat and limp french fries in three gulps.

"Man!" said Eddie as he slammed his tray down next to Hec's. "How can you eat that stuff? It looks like cow barf."

"I was hungry," Hec said through a mouthful of powdery peas. Suddenly Hec stopped chewing. He had the eerie, hair-raising feeling that he was being watched, the same strange feeling he got when he watched old sci-fi movies late at night with the curtains open. Someone was standing very close behind him, practically breathing down his neck. Slowly, slowly, without moving his body he turned his head until he was staring right at a purple striped shirt. Hec was so surprised he nearly spit peas.

"Hi Hec," Sandy said.

"Uh," said Hec.

"I wanted to thank you for walking Callie home yesterday. That was really sweet."

"Uh," said Hec.

"Here. I made these myself." Sandy pressed a baggie into Hec's hand, then disappeared into the lunchroom crowd.

"Uh," said Hec.

"That's my buddy, the brilliant conversationalist. So, what'd she give you?" Eddie asked. Hec looked at the baggie. It was full of funny, lumpy cookies dotted with M&Ms. Some had blackened bottoms. Some were crushed and crumbly. But all of them had been made by Sandy. They were the most beautiful cookies Hec had ever seen.

"Cool! Gimme one," Eddie lunged at the cookies, but Hec clutched the bag to his chest. He glared at Eddie.

"No one's going to eat these cookies, not ever," Hec said. Suddenly he had an idea. A brilliant idea. Hec scurried out of the lunchroom like a knight on a holy quest, for he knew exactly what to give Sandy.

Chapter Six

Hec marched to the student council snack bar. He set his cookies on the counter so he could shove his hand into his pocket. "Twelve packs of M&Ms, please," he said.

Mrs. Darling, the guidance counselor, was tending the snack bar. She peered over the top of her little half glasses and her nostrils flared in disapproval. Hec wondered if she, too, was really some kind of alien invader. She certainly had never been a teenager herself.

"And you're going to pay for them with that?" She reached for the baggie, but Hec lurched forward and grabbed it.

"No ma'am! I've got money!" He slapped the remainder of the lunch money Mom had given him on the counter. All six dollars of it.

"Surely you don't plan to eat all twelve packages, Hector," said Mrs. Darling.

"No ma'am!" Hec shoved the pile of crumpled bills forward.

"You're not buying for all your friends? You know you can't buy friendship, don't you?"

35

"No ma'am. They're for a project I saw in a Martha Stewart magazine."

Mrs. Darling leaned over the counter and gave Hec an alien death stare. "You expect me to believe that you read Martha Stewart magazines, Hector? What are you really planning to do with these M&Ms? Shoot them from straws? Pretend they're pills and swallow them whole? Crush them in the bleachers? Drool in Technicolor during biology? Go ahead and tell me: I've heard it all before."

"Really!" Hec's voice cracked so many times the word came out as four syllables in four different octaves. "My mom sometimes leaves her magazines in the bathroom so I look at them when I'm . . ." Hec's voice cracked like static on a short wave radio. This was not the sort of thing he was used to talking about with women. He decided to skip the gory details and get right to the important part. "I'm gonna make roses with chopsticks. Uhm, in a basket. These are the centers. And there's tissue paper petals!"

Mrs. Darling shook her head and handed over the candies. "Honestly, Hector. If you used half this much brainpower on your homework you'd be at Harvard by now, a child prodigy on a full scholarship." But Hec wasn't listening. He had his candies and was plotting his next step.

When Hec met Chloe coming up the front walk after school, he was still clutching his baggie and twelve bags of M&Ms to his chest. Chloe walked with the same man-on-a-mission determination as he did. She carried a little plastic bag from the drugstore clutched to her chest in the same manner. It was all very un-Chloe-like.

"Hi, Chloe. What's in the bag?" Hec asked.

"None of your business. What's in yours?" she responded.

"None of your business." They came through the front door shoulder to shoulder, both bursting with intensity.

"Hi, sweeties! Want some popcorn?" Mom called from the kitchen.

"Not now! I'm going to the bathroom," Chloe called and leaped up the stairs two at a time.

"Not now! Got any chopsticks?" Hec dropped his bag on the kitchen counter and rummaged through the junk drawer. He found a roll of tape, which he stuck in his pocket, a half dozen candle stubs, a bazillion rubber bands, and half a hardened granola bar, but no chopsticks.

"They're in the attic, in the house decoration box marked 'Chinese New Year,'" Mom said. "What are you and your sister up to?"

"I dunno about Chloe. I've got a little project to do. Got any red or pink tissue paper? How about an old basket? Florist foam?"

"Tissue paper in the wrapping paper box under my bed. Old baskets out in the garage. Florist foam next to the hot glue gun on the top shelf in the laundry room. What long, wide strip of the tissue paper with one straight side and one wavy side. He laid the strip on the floor, placed the M&M bag on top of it with the stick sticking out the straight side, then began rolling the bag along the tissue. When he came to the end of the tissue he taped the straight side onto the stick. Voilá! A perfect tissue paper rose with a bag of M&Ms in the center. Well, ok, he admitted. Not perfect, but at least he could tell it was supposed to be a rose. He made eleven more, rammed them into the florist foam in the bottom of the basket, then stood back to look at his handiwork. The basket tipped over. He stood it up. It dropped over again.

"Rats," Hec muttered. He pulled the shoebox containing his rock collection out from under his bed and stuffed a hunk of rose quartz into the foam on the light side. The basket stood. Hec let out a sigh. It looked pretty good. Suddenly he realized how hungry he was.

Hec wandered back to the kitchen. He rubbed Stevie's fuzzy blond head and dropped into a kitchen chair. Stevie's tongue stuck out of the side of his mouth. He signed his name on another of the stack of Cosmic Demon Valentine's cards.

"Will you wite a balemtime for me?" Stevie asked.

"Sure, sport. What do you want it to say?"

"Woses are wed, biwets are bwue, I wish I could shoot you wif a bazooka."

"Stevie, honey, that's not nice!" Mom said.

"It's for Emily. She wikes me," Stevie said.

"I'll take that snack now," Hec said to Mom, who was stirring a pot at the stove.

"There it is. Help yourself. I'm making tuna casserole. Your Father's favorite." She pointed a steaming wooden spoon at the basket of popcorn on the table. Hec looked at Mom. The funny plastic curlers no longer gave him the shock they used to, and he kind of liked the fuzzy pink sweater she was wearing.

"That new sweater looks nice," Hec said, stuffing his mouth with popcorn. Just then Chloe entered the kitchen. Hec spluttered and coughed, sending a mini-snowstorm of popcorn particles flying. Chloe's hair, while still purple tinged, was curled. The black eyeliner was gone, replaced by soft purple eye shadow. Her cheeks glowed pale pink, and frosty pink lipstick coated her lips. She wore a purple sweater instead of her usual black one.

"Speaking of looking nice," Mom said with a smile. "Isn't that the sweater Aunt Caroline sent you? I don't think you've ever worn it before."

Chloe blushed. "There's a first time for everything. Spring's a good time to change your look." She pulled a carrot from the fridge and nibbled at it as delicately as a rabbit. Hec wondered if she was being careful so she wouldn't smudge her lipstick.

"You wook̲s ̲il̲

surely go back to looking like Miss Gloom and Doom of 1348.

The front door slammed and Calvin trudged wearily into the kitchen. "What a day!" he sighed. "I need a tall, frosty glass of milk. Better make it a double." After months of hearing Mr. Buttons do all the speaking for him, the sound of Calvin's voice was a bit strange.

Mom stared at her middle son. "Calvin, are you alright? Where's Mr. Buttons?"

"In my backpack, the traitor," Calvin growled into his milk.

DING DONG!

Before he could explain further, the doorbell rang. Stevie and Hec scrambled out of their seats, but Calvin remained cradling his drink. "If it's for me, I'm not home," he shouted.

Callie smiled sweetly when Hec opened the door. "Hi Hec nice to see you again is Calvin home?" she blurted, with no breaths or pauses.

"Sorry," Hec answered. "He says he's not in." He shut the door.

DING DONG!

He opened the door. This time Callie had a little girl sock puppet on her hand. It had red yarn hair, and two blue buttons for eyes.

"Is Mr. Buttons at home?" it asked in a squeaky voice. "Tell him it's Suzie Stitches."

Hec heard Calvin groan in the other room. "Can you wait a minute? I'll check," he said and pushed the door closed.

"How could he do this to me?" Calvin said, pulling Mr. Buttons out of his pack. "Fall in love with a wild redhead and drag me into it! It's embarrassing."

"Why don't you just tell Mr. Buttons he can't see Suzie Stitches?" Hec asked.

"You try telling him. He has a mind of his own," Calvin said. He slid his puppet onto his hand. Calvin's voice changed back into the irritatingly high voice of Mr. Buttons. "Coming, my little sock'o love!" he called, and disappeared out the front door.

Chapter Seven

Hec used Chloe's blow dryer to unsteam the bathroom mirror. This physical hygiene thing was such a pain. You take a shower. You shampoo your hair. Apply deodorant. Put on fresh underwear and socks. And a week later you have to do the whole thing over again. Who had time for such nonsense?

Once he'd blasted a clear spot on the mirror he picked up a comb and tried to tame the unruly knot that was his hair. Calvin had straight hair. Stevie's peach fuzz wasn't long, but it was straight. Chloe and Mom's hair was stick-straight. Why had he inherited Dad's froth of curls? It reminded him of Larry from The Three Stooges. Hec drew the comb down the side of his head, trying to force a part, but the hair just curled right back over. It was like trying to part water.

cute, either. Nothing special about his lips. He had the most boring, nondescript face known to mankind.

Very well. If he couldn't impress Sandy with his looks, he would dazzle her with his wit and charm. He leaned toward the mirror and flashed a debonair smile. "For you," he said, holding out the flower basket. Hec smiled and studied his teeth. If he was going to impress her with his smile maybe he should brush the yellow fuzzy stuff off his teeth.

He put on his Sunday best black pants and his white, button-down shirt. He carefully studied his two ties and selected the gray and brown print one. He concentrated, his tongue sticking out the side of his mouth, and tied it around his neck. Rats. The thin end hung a good eight inches past the thick end. Hec pulled it loose and tried again. This time the thick end was long enough to sit on. Hec tried three more times but just couldn't get it right. He took the pot of flowers and the tie and marched down to the laundry room, where he could hear his mom humming as she folded laundry. Mom had those weird plastic curlers on again. He noticed her pink sweater, her capri pants, and the strappy little sandals with the clear plastic heels. They were quite a bit different from her usual sweats and sneakers.

"Can you tie this for me?" he asked.

Mom looked up. She raised an eyebrow. "What's up, honey bunny?"

"Oh, nothing. I've got a delivery to make," Hec said as casually as he could. Mom smiled and asked no more questions, for which he was grateful. Sometimes it was just too hard to explain things. Mom seemed to know that this was one of those times. He tucked the flower basket under his arm like a football and headed up the street.

Old Lady McLarty stood up as Hec passed her house. He could hear her back creak all the way from the sidewalk. "What are you up to this time, you young whippersnapper?" she demanded.

"Nothing, Mrs. McLarty," answered Hec.

She put her fists on her ample hips and gave a great harrumph. "Don't 'nothing' me, boy! I can tell you're up to no good! I can tell a boy who's courting and sparking a mile off. Don't you push that sweet young thing into anything that would sully her." Hec let out a little nervous laugh. Apparently Old Lady McLarty thought more of his courting abilities than Hec did.

Calvin and Callie sat on the front steps of the Richardson house. Mr. Buttons' and Suzie Stitches' sock-covered heads leaned close together while Callie's and Calvin's other hands held dripping Popsicles.

"What'cha doing, Hec?" Mr. Buttons asked in his little squeaky voice.

"Mind your own beeswax," Hec said. He leaned over Calvin's head and pushed the doorbell. 'She'll be Coming 'Round the Mountain' chimed away, accompanied by the

Skitter,

yip!

yip!

yip!,

thump !

of Sandy's dog.

"Sandy's got a boyfriend! Sandy's got a boyfriend!" Suzie Stitches teased. Mr. Buttons joined in, making it a duet. Hec glanced up. Old Lady McLarty leaned against the fence, fixing him with her best alien death stare. He could feel the tie tightening around his neck, feel sweat dripping down his back.

"Coming!" Sandy called from inside.

Suddenly Hec panicked. He shoved the basket into Calvin's lap. "You give it to her," he blurted and ran back down the street, his tie waving goodbye over his shoulder.

By the time Hec got home, his hair stood back from his sweaty red forehead as if he'd been going warp ten in a Tai Fighter. He collapsed onto the sofa just as Mom walked past with a laundry basket.

"You ok, honey bunny?" she asked.

"As ok as an idiot can be," he groaned. Mom put an arm around his shoulder, squeezing him

46

tight. Her curlers pressed into the side of his head. Yoicks, they hurt. How could Mom stand wearing those instruments of torture?

"Want to talk about it?" she asked.

Hec shook his head and shrugged. What was there to talk about? And what would a Mom know about pleasing girls?

"After all, I was a teenage girl once," Mom said.

Hec shivered. It gave him the willies when she read his mind like that. Maybe women, especially Moms, were from Venus after all.

Mom stood back up and balanced the laundry basket on her hip. "I'll be upstairs when you're ready to talk," she said. He closed his eyes and wished the world would go away, but it wouldn't. Mom's little plastic heels click-clicked up the wooden stairs. Off in the distance, Hec heard a distinctive

PING, ZIP, POP.

Stevie was playing Space Invaders on the computer. Mom hummed as she opened drawers to put away laundry. Hec heard her go into Chloe's room. Two female voices tell door and his stereo sounded louder, then faded again when she closed the door behind her. It became silent upstairs, so that all Hec could hear was Stevie bringing the alien invaders to their knees. Hec strained to figure out what Mom was doing, but he heard nothing. He cracked open one eye. The empty laundry basket stood at the top of the stairs but Mom was nowhere in sight.

Hec peeled himself off the sofa and trudged upstairs. "Mom?" he whined. His voice sounded lonely and distant, as if he was the only living soul on the planet.

"Hmmm?" Mom's voice came from somewhere near her bedroom.

Hec took a step closer. "Mom?" he called again.

"Hmmm?" Mom answered. Like echolocation, Hec kept calling 'Mom' and she kept 'hmmming' until he found her. She was standing at her bathroom counter, pulling plasticy Velcro rollers out of her hair and tossing them into the sink.

Hec slumped down on the side of the bathtub and let out a great sigh. "There's this new girl in school," he started. "She's really pretty, and she's really nice, too. I like her a lot, but every time I get close to her I make a mess of it. She must think I'm the biggest fool on the entire planet."

"What kind of mess, honey bunny?"

"The first time I met her, I dumped my entire backpack all over the math class floor. The second time, I ran away. Then I ran my bike into Eddie's mailbox – right in front of her! I thought I really had it together this time. I made this really nice present, got all dressed up, practiced my lines, then at the last minute I freaked and ran down the street as if an alien slime monster was after me. I bet she's still rolling around laughing."

"I bet not." Mom winced and pulled out another roller. "She's probably sorry for how hard this is for you. Girls don't like to cause pain. Really we don't."

Hec sighed. He wished he believed that. Yet again, hadn't Sandy been more than nice? She'd made him cookies. She'd smiled at him. She'd handed him his pencil the first day. But maybe that was all before she realized what a dork he was.

"Maybe you're trying too hard," Mom said as she dropped another roller in the sink.

"What do you mean?"

"I mean, why don't you just be yourself. Forget the tie and the Sunday best clothes. Flowers are nice, but so is a nice smile and a hello. She's not some alien from outer space, you know."

Hec picked up a roller and twirled it on the end of his finger. "You mean, like you?"

Mom stopped pulling her hair out with the rollers and looked at Hec. "Are you saying I'm trying too hard, or are you saying that I'm acting like an alien?"

the down to earth, cookies and milk kind of mom. Suddenly you're the glamour queen."

Mom sighed and sat down next to Hec on the side of the bathtub. "This whole boy/girl stuff is complicated, isn't it, sweetie?"

"You said it," Hec sighed, and together they stared at the bathroom floor without speaking for a long, long time.

Chapter Eight

Hec heard his bedroom door open. Someone flicked off his droning alarm. The bed tilted as someone sat. He wished he were dreaming, but knew he wasn't. He wished there was something – anything – to distract him from cold, hard reality. The cold, hard reality was, it was time to get up. He did not want to start another day – another chance to make a complete fool out of himself. It was safer to stay in bed.

"Good morning, honey bunny." Mom bobbed up and down, making the bed gently rock. Hec opened one eye. She was still wearing her silly new zebra robe, but her hair was back in a ponytail instead of rollers. He waved one limp hand so she'd know he was awake.

"I've been thinking," Mom said. "That was an awfully sweet thing you did yesterd   Mak g all those paper roses. San ly can't but e impressed."

Hec sat up and scratched his   "You think?"

"I do. And even if you didn't present them in person, you did put on a tie, and you walked all the way over there. I bet Sandy will say 'thank you' today."

"Great. I've set myself up for another disaster." Hec tried to sound cynical but Mom's words had filled him with a strange euphoria.

"You'd better be ready. Figure out now what you're going to say." Mom gave Hec's back a good, sound thumping for encouragement. She was almost out the door when Hec called to her.

"So, what'll I say?" he asked.

Mom turned back. She gave him a little smile. "How about 'you're welcome,'" she said, and she was gone.

Stevie was eating Cheerios with a toothpick when Hec came down for breakfast. "Why'd you take a shower? It's not Sunday."

Hec's hair dripped all over the sports page. Why didn't he ever remember to towel it dry? "You're welcome," he answered in his deepest voice. Even though it didn't answer Stevie's question, it was good practice. "What's the count?"

"A hunnert and twenny-one days, and two days 'til da dentist," Stevie answered.

"Hec's got a girlfriend! Hec's got a girlfriend!" Mr. Buttons sang.

"Calvin's got one, too! Calvin's got one, too!" Hec sang back.

Calvin pulled Mr. Buttons off his hand and threw him across the room. "I do not!" he shouted in his regular Calvin voice. "Girls are yucky!"

"Then why were you over at Callie's yesterday?" Hec knew it wasn't nice to tease his brother, but it sure was fun.

"'Cause her gived him pocsicles," Stevie said.

"I don't like popsicles! They're full of girl germs! It's not my fault Mr. Buttons likes Suzie Stitches," Calvin protested.

"You're the one who took me over," Mr. Buttons protested from across the room. Hec gawked. He didn't know Calvin could throw his voice so far.

"You keep out of this," Calvin shouted to the puppet. He walked over and picked Mr. Buttons back up.

"Don't you blame me for your behavior. You know you like Callie but you're afraid to admit it." Mr. Buttons shook his little sock hand at Calvin. Hec could swear the puppet made a fist.

"Don't tell me what I know!" Calvin shouted back.

Hec shook his head. This was too weird.

Mom looked over the top of the editorials page. "That's enough. Stop it, you two. Now apologize to each other or I'll ground you both."

Calvin and Mr. Buttons muttered apologies and Calvin went back to eating Cocoa Crunchies.

"You're welcome," Hec recited again.

"Morning!" Chloe said perkily. Her hair was curled, and she was still wearing that pretty pink lipstick. This morning's shirt was sunny yellow, which clashed a bit with her hair. She pulled a yogurt from the fridge and dropped into her seat.

"Where's Dad?" she asked, looking at his empty place.

Mom set down the paper. "Your father's working awful hours. They keep postponing the project, which means Dad stands around for hours, doing nothing, waiting for something to happen. We were already asleep when he got in last night. This morning he got up really early and left before five."

"That means he hasn't seen your new clothes," Chloe said. Her voice was uncharacteristically full of sympathy instead of judgment. "Oh Mom, it's such a pity. You're trying so hard to please him and he's not even around to notice. I hope the person who sent me flowers notices – and appreciates – my new look."

"I'm sure they do, honey bunny." Mom took a big sip of coffee, "But you know, you don't have to change just to please someone else."

Hec shook his head. Did either his mother or his sister actually listen to themselves?

Eddie was sitting on the curb with his head in his hands when Hec came out. It was a frosty morning, much too cold to be sitting on curbs. Something was wrong.

"Hey buddy, what's up?" Hec punched Eddie's arm. Hard.

Eddie gave a wry smile as he rubbed the sore spot. "I'm a victim of my own genius," he said.

Hec chuckled. Eddie had a quick wit. He was always and forever coming up with clever schemes. He was often his own worst enemy. "I take it the flower thing didn't go over well."

"Man, Hec! I'll say! I sent flowers to Tia Maria's house. To be on the safe side, I sent some to Mom's office, too. Mom showed up last night, all bubbly and silly."

"Like Chloe. Flowers are for women what catnip is for cats," Hec noted.

"Whatever. Anyway, Dad denied everything. He guessed some other guy sent them. Things were spiraling out of control, so I stepped in and confessed." Eddie drew his hands through his hair, making it wilder than ever. It looked like a confused sea urchin had taken up residence atop Eddie's head.

"That should have helped," Hec said.

"Should have. Didn't. They started pointing fingers and accusing each other of raising a shiftless, meddlesome, credit card thieving delinquent."

Ouch. Whoever said 'sticks and stones can break my bones but words will never hurt me' hadn't been called anything like that. Not by his own parents. They marched on in silence for quite a while.

"YOU'RE welcome. You're WELcome. You're WELCOME," Hec practiced putting the emphasis on a different syllable each time.

Eddie looked askance at Hec. "What's that all about?"

"Just practicing," answered Hec. He hoped he'd get the chance to use it.

Chapter Nine

Sandy didn't say a word to Hec in Mr. Grumbolt's class. She didn't even look at him, even when he tripped over Wes Snyder's outstretched leg, dumping his backpack all over the aisle. Once, he thought she started to turn her head his direction, but he was sure she'd blushed and purposefully turned away. He felt like the wind had been knocked out of him. The empty pain in his stomach was worse than hitting Eddie's mailbox. Had he blown it forever? Which had embarrassed her more, his stupid flower basket or his behavior? Would she ever speak to him again? Just in case, he muttered "You're welcome" over and over between each class.

At lunch, Eddie and Hec sullenly sat side-by-side at a cafeteria table, glumly picking at their food. Neither had an appetite. Hec scanned the cafeteria. Wes Snyder, the center for the basketball team and the tallest, most popular kid in the school was holding court with his admirers in the center of the cafeteria. Wes tossed a roll, bouncing it off the top of a little six grader's head

57

and his crowd roared approvingly. Hec shook his head. Why did someone so popular have to treat everyone else so badly?

Hec scanned the room some more and found Sandy sitting with a gaggle of girls on the far side. He could tell she wasn't looking for him. Probably wasn't even thinking of him. He felt like the incredible invisible man.

Eddie's eyes followed Hec's. "Phooey," he said. "Phooey on girls. Phooey on love." He stirred chocolate milk into his mashed potatoes, took a bite of his concoction, and made a face. "Phooey on these potatoes!" He pushed his tray away and held his hand up as if testifying in court. "Man, Hec, I've had it! From this day forward I vow to have nothing to do with girls, love, or cafeteria potatoes."

"I dunno," Hec answered. "If you add enough chocolate milk, these potatoes aren't so bad."

Eddie punched Hec's arm. "Phooey! My luck's gotta change sometime. I'm going to the game card shop after school. Maybe I'll buy a deck with a valuable card for once. Wanna go?"

"Nah. I'm not feeling lucky. You go. I'll just go home," Hec replied.

The walk home was long and lonely. Not that it really was. With or without his buddy, the distance remained the same half-mile. It just seemed longer without Eddie's jokes. Hec wasn't alone, either. The sidewalk was full of other students. But none of them was Eddie. They'd been best friends since kindergarten. Some days, though, a guy just needed to be alone with his thoughts.

Hec still felt like the incredible invisible man, walking along with everyone else, yet cut off from all of them. Astronauts wear special suits to insulate them from harsh environments. Hec felt insulated, but was the harsh environment out there, or inside him? Was he sealed off to protect himself from the world, or to protect the world from him?

"Hec?"

WHOOP! WHOOP! WHOOP!

The voice set off Hec's mental warning system.

Sandy blushed and smiled as he waited for her to catch up. "I'm glad I found you. I've wanted to talk to you all day, but I thought we could talk better without the whole math class listening.

"Uh," Hec replied.

"That bouquet was really thoughtful. I can tell you worked hard on it. M&Ms are my favorite."

"You're welcome," he answered. His voice cracked so many times it sounded like radio static. And after all that practice! 'Beam me up, Scotty,' he thought. 'I'm showing no intelligent life here. Better yet, blast me to bits.'

Sandy giggled. "I'm sorry, Hec. I know I shouldn't laugh, but it's so cute when your voice does that."

"Cute?" Hec blurted in disbelief.

"Yeah, cute. I like the way your eyebrows come together when it happens. You take everything so seriously! I guess you brainy, scientist types are like that."

Hec swallowed. "I've got a confession," he said. His voice cracked three times but he didn't mind. Not if Sandy thought it was cute. "I'm not that brainy. Eddie and I aren't really doing a project on quantum physics."

"But you could if you wanted to. I can tell you're really smart. Here's your street. See you tomorrow."

Really? Smart? She thought he was really smart? And cute? Street or no street, Hec didn't want this moment to end. "I'll walk you all the way home. Can I carry your books?" Hec let his voice joyously skip and jump through four octaves.

"Thanks, but they're in my backpack," Sandy said.

"I'll carry your backpack, then." Hec gallantly put Sandy's pack right on top of his. It was quite a load – both awkward and heavy, but Hec felt as if he could run and win the Olympics – the entire Olympics – with them. In a space suit. And double gravity. Old Lady McLarty looked up as Sandy and Hec-the-sherpa passed. Her mouth hung open, and her gums flapped but she didn't say a word.

"Well, here we are," Sandy said when they reached her door. She turned and flashed a dimpled, dazzling smile.

Suddenly all of Hec's confidence evaporated.

WHOOP! WHOOP! WHOOP!

His brain screamed.

"Uh," he said.

"Thanks for carrying my backpack. And thanks again for the flowers. They're so pretty, I may never eat them."

"Uh." That wasn't what he was supposed to say. What was he supposed to say? Hec stared at her backpack, the doormat, a bush. Anything but Sandy.

"Are you going to the dance on Friday?" she asked.

"Uh."

"If you do, will you dance with me?"

Hec's heart lurched into warp speed. "You're welcome," he said.

Sandy laughed, but it was such a happy sound that he knew she wasn't laughing at him. "You are so funny, Hector Anderson! See you tomorrow!" She slipped inside, flashed him one more brilliant smile, then closed the door.

"Now there's a nice boy," Old Lady McLarty said aloud to herself as he passed by. "He carries girls' books for them."

Hec's chest puffed with pride. That's right. Hector Anderson was the cutest, smartest, most gentlemanly 13-year-old boy on the face of planet Earth. He cruised home, his feet just barely skimming the ground as he soared on booster rockets of joy.

Chapter Ten

Hec and Eddie were playing basketball in Eddie's driveway after school on Thursday when Eddie's mom drove up. Mrs. Hernandez slammed the door of her Jaguar and tack, tack, tacked up the walkway as fast as her high heels would allow.

"Hi, Mrs. Hernandez," Hec said as he passed the ball to Eddie.

"Hi, Mike," she answered without even looking at him.

Eddie stopped dribbling and stared at his mother. "That's not Mike. That's Hec, my best friend."

"It's hard to keep all your little friends separate," she said, dismissing the subject with a wave of her hand. "Eddie, get packed. You're spending the weekend with me."

"I'll help!" Hec offered. He followed Eddie and his mom into the house. They clattered back to Eddie's room, where Mrs. Hernandez grabbed a duffel and began stuffing Eddie's clothes in.

Jennifer Bohnhoff

"Let's see, you'll need Friday, Saturday, Sunday, Monday, four pairs of underwear," she said to herself as she rifled through his drawers.

"Does Dad know about this?" Eddie asked.

She rolled three T-shirts and stuffed them in the bag. "He will when he sees the note we leave."

"Uh, Mom, the weekend doesn't start until tomorrow."

"I know. I thought we'd get a jump on it." His mom stuffed a side pocket full of socks.

"But Dad was going to take me fishing!"

Mrs. Hernandez stopped packing long enough to fix Eddie with her eyes. "I know," she said. "Why do you think we're going to San Antonio? Six Flags Over Texas, the Alamo, the beach. We're going to have fun."

Eddie rubbed his chin. "Ohhh, I get it. Custody battle. Let's see which parent I pick. Well, Mom, I'm on to you. You can't buy my loyalty with a trip to Texas. You'll have to do way better than that."

His mom sighed. She sat down on the edge of the bed. "Disneyland?"

"And I get to take Hec," Eddie said.

"No way. One kid on a trip is plenty," Mom crossed her arms and looked determined.

"Deal." Eddie and his mom shook on it. She zipped up his bag and went to the kitchen where she jotted a quick note.

"Sorry, Hec. Can't say I didn't try," Eddie said, slapping Hec on the back.

"What about the dance tomorrow?" Hec said as he followed them out the door.

Eddie tossed his duffel into the back seat and jumped in. He rolled down the window as the engine hummed to life. "Save a cookie for me! Bye!"

Hec came into his room to find Stevie siting amid crumbs on his bed, an empty baggie in his hand.

"What are you doing?" Hec snatched the baggie and clutched it tightly.

"Eating cookies. Tomowwow I has to go to da dentist." He pounded his fist into his chest in the Roman gladiator salute. "Me, who are about to die sawoot you."

"Those were the sacred Sandy cookies!"

"And dey weren't vewy good."

Hec felt like the top of his head was going to blow off in an eruption. "You little rat! I hope your teeth rot out! Out! Before I pound you into pulp!"

"Aww, Hec. Dey was onwy cookies," Stevie whined.

Hec threw himself face down amongst the scattered crumbs. They stuck to his skin. Crumbs. That was all that was left. The greatest present he had ever received reduced to nothing but crumbs. Life wasn't fair.

"What do you think?" Chloe waited to twirl around until Hec looked at her. Her pink skirt billowed out, looking as light and fluffy as cotton candy.

"Great," Hec said, dropping his face back into the crumbs.

65

"You sure?" Chloe asked. When Hec didn't answer, she dropped down next to him on the bed and stroked his back. "Mom got it for me, for the dance. You're still going to yours aren't you? You seem kind of blue."

"Eddie's not going," Hec answered. He rolled onto his back and stared at the ceiling.

"So? You weren't going to dance with Eddie."

"Chloe, you still don't know who sent you those roses, do you?"

"Of course not, silly. But I'm sure he'll make himself known at the dance."

"What if he's someone you don't like? What if he's some stupid dork who constantly does stupid things? Will you hate him, then, for getting your hopes up?"

Chloe was silent for a long time, thinking, Hec supposed, about the possibilities. "I guess I'll be disappointed," she finally admitted. "But hate him? I'll still be grateful for how he's made me feel. Knowing that someone out there cares has been wonderful. I've grown and matured as a person. I've stretched my boundaries. I owe him a great debt of gratitude."

"Gratitude for what?" Calvin asked as he walked into Hec's bedroom. It was like Grand Central Station in here. Couldn't the world leave a guy and his crumbs alone in their misery?

"Where's Mr. Buttons?" Chloe asked.

"In the toy box," Calvin muttered. "All that sweet talk and Popsicles! It was getting to me. Then Suzie Stitches asked Mr. Buttons to marry her and I just couldn't take it anymore." He

66

sighed and dropped down on the bed. His bouncing imbedded crumbs deeper in Hec's cheek. Calvin picked one up, sniffed it and stuck it in his mouth. Hec didn't even protest. Crumbs. His world reduced to crumbs.

"This cookie is yucky," Calvin muttered. So's this love stuff."

"No it's not. It's wonderful," Chloe argued.

Hec didn't know who to believe.

Chapter Eleven

Hec tugged at the collar of his polo shirt as if it was an alien tentacle choking him. He wanted to rip the stupid shirt off and stuff it in the trash can in the boy's bathroom, but the principal didn't allow students to walk around half-naked. Anyway, not wearing a shirt would make him even more self-conscious than wearing this one.

Hec hated this shirt. Especially the color. Mom said the pale powder blue brought out the color of his eyes. Hec thought it made him look like a baby. It was bad enough to have to wear it on Sundays. Leave it to Mom to insist he wear it to the dance. Wearing it all day long reminded him that the dance was after school. Why didn't they give a kid time to go home, take a shower and put on fresh clothes? Hec knew the answer: few kids could come back. He sure wouldn't. At least he had his sacred Sandy cookie bag, complete with crumbs, in his pocket for good luck.

The Student Council had made a rather disheartened attempt to decorate the cafeteria. Someone had taped black paper over the windows, which made the room look more dreary than dark. The tables were folded up and stacked in one corner. A few straggly streamers and some bunches of limp balloons hung from the rafters. The odd assortment of posters touting the virtues of hand washing and the importance of the food pyramid didn't add to the atmosphere.

Hec took a deep breath and stepped in. What should he do? Where should he go? What did a guy do at a dance? No one was dancing. Most of the boys clustered around the refreshment table straight across the room. He couldn't walk through the middle of the room. Not without attracting attention. Little knots of girls giggled together on the left. Was Sandy among them? In the twilight he couldn't see, at least not without looking like he was looking. Better not go there. At his right was the afternoon's entertainment, Student Council President Mike Morgan with his giant boom box pounding out bubblegum pop by the Handsome Brothers. No one was dancing. Beyond Mike, in the distant, dark corner, Hec's math teacher, Mr. Grumbolt sat crunched in a student desk, looking like an NBA player in a preschool chair. The safest way to get to the cookies and punch was past Mr. Grumbolt. Hec stuck his hands in his pockets and nonchalantly strolled around the edge of the room. Mr. Grumbolt's red pen hovered over a stack of math quizzes, ready to pounce on a wrong answer.

"Hi, Mr. Grumbolt," Hec said.

The math teacher raised his bushy eyebrows above his gold frame glasses. His mustache drooped over his mouth so much that Hec couldn't tell whether or not he was frowning. "Hi yourself, Hector. Come to do a little dancing?"

"I think I'm here for the cookies," Hec said. "Some of the PTA moms make really good cookies."

"I'm here because the principal told me I had to chaperone. Let me know if there's a fight," Mr. Grumbolt scratched his stubbly chin like he did when thinking up a particularly difficult question to ask. "PTA mom cookies, huh? Bring me back some would you?"

Hec crossed the no-mans'-land between Mr. Grumbolt's dark corner and the refreshment table. At least he had something to do. He slapped hands with a few of the boys who slouched against the wall. He smiled at Mrs. Darling, the guidance counselor, who was now serving punch, then scanned the trays. On the third tray from the end, he spied lumpy, slightly blackened cookies studded with M&Ms. Hec's heart fluttered. This must be how prince charming felt when he found the other glass slipper! Hec pulled the baggie out of his pocket and filled it with cookies.

"Ah, ah, ah," Ms. Darling said as she wagged a finger. "Let's not be piggy."

"These are for Mr. Grumbolt. He asked me to bring him some," Hec said, palming a few Oreos. He jerked his chin toward the math teacher.

"Oh. I see. Well, we'd better take him some punch then, too." She handed Hec two Dixie cups dripping with red, sticky stuff and stuffed a couple of napkins into his pocket.

"Thanks, Hec," Mr. Grumbolt said as Hec set down a cup and the Oreos. "That's awfully nice of you, especially when I didn't even offer you any extra credit."

Hec wasn't sure, but he thought he saw a bit of a smile amid the mustache.

"You're welcome. It gave me something to do," Hec said, looking around. Hec swore he could hear the scritch, scratch as Mr. Grumbolt rubbed his chin.

"If you're looking for something to do, I suggest you ask Sandy to dance," Mr. Grumbolt said.

Hec felt like one of those characters in the cartoons whose eyes pop out in surprise. "Sandy? Dance?" His voice danced through three octaves.

Mr. Grumbolt set down his pen. "It's clear you like her, Hec. You've done nothing in math class all week but stare at the side of her head. And judging by how she blushes, I think she likes you, too."

"She's here?" The alien tentacle collar felt twice as tight. A bead of sweat trickled down his spine.

WHOOP! WHOOP! WHOOP!

His mental alert siren was drowning out Mike Morgan's boom box.

Mr. Grumbolt gestured with his pen to a point behind Hec. "Right over there. She's wearing a dress that matches your shirt. You two even look like you belong together."

Hec slowly turned. Act casual, he thought, but it was hard to act casual with his heart pounding in his ears and his knees turning to rubber.

"At least go talk to her." Mr. Grumbolt leaned forward and gave Hec a sly grin. "I'll give you extra credit."

Hec took a deep breath. He patted the baggie in his pocket for reassurance and walked into the center of the room. The dance floor was as barren as the moon. Hec felt like an astronaut crossing it. Every eye in the room was on him. The gaggle of girls stopped talking. Hec was almost to the halfway point when he began to lose his nerve.

WHOOP! WHOOP! WHOOP!

How could he let a teacher use the promise of extra credit to lure him into such a stupid stunt? He was just about to make a sharp right and head toward the refreshment table when Sandy stepped out of the gaggle and smiled at him.

Hec's feet quit moving. Sandy. Smiled. At him. Suddenly it didn't matter what music Mike Morgan played. It didn't matter that he was in a cafeteria with blacked –out windows and limp balloons. It didn't matter that everyone was looking at him. Everything was perfect. Hec smiled back.

A movement near the cafeteria door pulled everyone's eyes from Hec. Hec turned, and the showdown began. There in the doorway, wearing his basketball uniform, stood Wesley Snyder. The entire team stood behind him, as if backing him up. Wesley glanced around the room. He sized up Hec. A sneer twisted his lips. His gaze fell on Sandy. The sneer turned into a leer. Hec's heart pounded as Wesley turned slowly back toward him. The sneer turned mean. Wesley raised one eyebrow and took a step toward Sandy.

Hec didn't need alien mind reading powers to know what Wesley was up to. Without saying a word, he'd said, "Sandy's mine and you stay away." He had his reputation, his uniform and his team to back him up. Hec glared defiantly at the star of the basketball team and took a step forward. Wesley's eyebrows arced. Like a boy playing Mother May I , Wesley took a giant step toward Sandy, then grinned back at Hec.

Any reasonable boy would have run away like a defeated Martian, gone to the refreshment table, and drowned his sorrows in red punch. But Hec was no longer reasonable. Instead of retreating, Hec took two steps forward.

Wesley reeled back as if he'd been struck, then took three baby steps and a hop toward Sandy. Hec responded with five giant steps. Wesley stomped his foot in exasperation and began to walk – slowly and methodically, but without stopping. Hec matched him step for step. Wesley broke into a run, the entire team following in drill formation. Hec matched the pace.

Hec was about to launch into warp speed when he heard a clickety clickety click behind him.

"Hi honey bunny! Having fun?" Hec whirled around, Sandy and Wesley forgotten with the sound of his mother's voice. Mom hobbled up to him, the skinny heels of her sandals clicketing across the floor. She wore her new pink sweater and her skinny Capri pants. Her hair was teased and sprayed 'til it defied gravity and stood out from her head like a space helmet.

"Mom," Hec groaned, "What are you doing here?"

"I volunteered to chaperone. Thought it'd be fun. Say, if this is a dance, why isn't anyone dancing?" she said, glancing around the room.

"People don't dance at dances," Hec said, but he knew it sounded lame as soon as he said it.

"Well, we'll just have to start something," she said. Mom clicketied across the floor with Hec scurrying along behind, issuing protests as he went. Mom ignored him. She stopped in front of Mr. Grumbolt's desk and put her hands on her hips.

"I thought I told you not to bother me unless there was a fight," Mr. Grumbolt said as he continued to grade papers. He looked up and his scowl melted. For a moment he sat with his face frozen in surprise, his pen poised above the paper. Quickly he dislodged himself from the tiny desk and came to his feet. "Excuse me," he said. "I thought you were a kid."

Mom's hands flew to her face. "How flattering!" she cooed. "I haven't been mistaken for a student for quite a while. I'm Veronica Anderson. Would you care to dance?"

"Mom!" Hec's voice went supersonic, but neither his mother nor his math teacher seemed to notice. They were already halfway to the dance floor.

Dance floor! Suddenly Hec remembered Sandy. He turned back to where she had been standing, but she was no longer there. He studied the gaggles. No Sandy. Hec searched the room with his eyes. The basketball team stood near the refreshment table. Wesley wasn't with them. Where could they be? Hec's eyes followed the team's gaze and finally rested on Wesley – together with Sandy – on the dance floor. Hec felt his stomach do a crash landing, as if an alien death beam had bored right through him.

Sandy looked over Wesley's shoulder. She smiled and gave a little wave – so small it was barely more than the fluttering of her fingers. But it was enough to boil Hec's blood. She'd chosen the most popular guy in school instead of, a geeky, unpopular nerd. Did she have to rub it in? It was all too much. He didn't want to see his mother dancing with his math teacher. He didn't want to see Sandy dancing with Wesley. Hec shoved his hands deep into his pockets and escaped the humiliation for the cool evening air.

Chapter Twelve

The evening air outside was crisp and clean. Hec took a deep, slow breath and tried to rid himself of the cafeteria images. Why did this sting so much? Why did he care who Sandy danced with, or Mom, for that matter? The sky turned purple and sapphire behind the blazing pink mountains.

"Oh, God, I wish things had turned out differently," he prayed silently. As if in answer, the first evening start twinkled faintly in the south.

Hec stuck his key in the front door. It was strange to come home to a deserted and dark house. Eddie did it all the time, but Hec was used to someone being home. That someone was usually Mom. Why did she have to be off at a dance, and in little high heels and a pink sweater?

"Anybody home?" he called. His voice seemed to echo in the loneliness.

"Right here," a deep voice answered. Hec's heart leaped. With trembling hands he flipped on the lamp and found Dad stretched out on the sofa.

77

He sat up and rubbed his face. "I came home to an empty house, so I thought I'd take a nap. Where is everybody?"

"Chloe's at a school dance. Mom's chaperoning the dance at my school. I don't know where the boys are." Hec plopped down next to his dad.

"It's not like your mom to leave the boys behind," Dad said.

"She's been doing a lot of things that aren't like her," Hec answered. "It's like an alien has taken over her body – an alien with high heels and a curly hairdo. She hasn't been herself ever since you forgot your anniversary."

"I haven't forgotten our anniversary," said Dad. "I have a gift and a card. After all, our anniversary's not until . . ." he looked at his watch and groaned, "last Monday. Heck, Hec, I've been so busy at the testing range that I lost track of time. But I didn't forget. It's hard, balancing work and family. I've really missed you guys this past week, and I've missed Mom most of all."

"So what'd you get her?" Hec asked. Not that he was really interested. It wouldn't be Dragons in the Midst playing cards or anything exciting. He heard Dad fumbling around in his bedroom drawers. Dad was coming back downstairs with a pearl necklace dangling from his fingers when a key rattled in the front door and Mom walked in. Her face was flushed as pink as her sweater and she was smiling. Dancing had done her good.

Hec wasn't sure which of his parents had the most surprised look.

"Wow, are you a sight for sore eyes! I'd forgotten how beautiful you are," Dad said.

Mom blushed even deeper and her hands flew to her throat. "Pearls! For me?" she said. Dad placed them around her neck, then spun her around and admired her.

"They don't do you justice," he murmured. Hec could tell that Mom wanted to say something, but the words didn't come, just a gush of happy tears. *Another happy ending for the Anderson family*, Hec thought. *I guess everything's going to be all right.*

Hec was about to leave his parents alone when the door crashed open and Chloe stomped in.

"Hi, honey bunny. How was your dance?" Mom asked.

Chloe's hands tightened into fists. She looked like a prizefighter in a pink puffy skirt. "Rotten," she said with a snort. "No one asked me to dance. No one even looked at me. I felt like a freak in a sideshow. Whoever sent me flowers, then left me high and dry at the dance, is going to pay for it!"

"Oh, Chloe, sweetie. I'm so sorry," Mom said. "It's all my fault." She wrapped her arms around her daughter and tried to hug her, but who can hug a rigid pole?

"You're not the guy who sent me flowers," Chloe said.

"I'm afraid I am," Mom answered. Chloe stared at Mom in shock. Her jaw moved up and down, but no words came out.

"You did?" Hec asked for his sister.

79

"I'm afraid so. You see, you seemed so sure that flowers and candy were worthless. I wanted to show you otherwise. I wanted you to know how it felt when someone thinks you're special enough to send you gifts."

Chloe's face went livid. "You tricked me!" she shouted. "You set me up for this disaster!" Her jaw worked as if she had more to say, but the horrible words wouldn't come out. Chloe burst into tears and flew up the stairs, slamming the door to her room behind her.

"Oh, Geoff," Mom groaned. "Look what I've done." She buried her face in her hands. Dad wrapped his arms around her and rocked her back and forth as if she were a child in need of comfort.

"You didn't mean to," Hec offered. "You had the best of intentions." Neither Dad nor Mom answered. Hec stood there for a few awkward moments, shuffling from foot to foot. He decided that sometimes the best thing to say is nothing at all, so he slid quietly out the front door and left Dad to console Mom alone.

It was truly dark outside now. A thousand stars twinkled in the black sky. Hec lay down in the frozen grass. He put his arms behind his head. He wished he were among the stars, out there in a spaceship all alone with no one to confuse his heart. The stars seemed so serene at this distance, so peaceful, so pure. Hec laughed a little sadly because he knew they only looked that way. They were really roiling, boiling balls of wildly violent gas. Appearances can be deceiving.

"Hec? Is that you?" Sandy's voice startled Hec. He jerked, but then lay still. If she'd come to rub it in, to get a reaction out of him, she was going to be disappointed.

"Yeah," he answered. His voice hardly cracked at all. Sandy sat down beside Hec in the grass. She pulled her jacket around her and gazed up. For a while they sat in silence. The longer the silence went on, the more uncomfortable Hec got. Why didn't she just get it over? It became clear that she wasn't going to shoot him down without a prompting. "So, did you have a good time at the dance?" he asked.

"Not really. Why did you abandon me?" Sandy said with a sigh. The question struck Hec as absurd.

"Abandon you? It looked to me like you were having a pretty good time."

"Dancing with Wesley? Yuck. I only danced with him because if I refused, his whole team would have made his life miserable. What a scene that would have been! Didn't you see me wave? I was hoping you'd save me, but you disappeared."

"I thought you were showing me how great you were for dancing with the most popular guy in school," Hec said. He wished he could take his words back the moment he'd said them. He didn't want to make Sandy appear mean, especially now that he knew she wasn't.

"Most popular guy in school? Wesley? Yuck. Hec, it doesn't take a degree in quantum physics to figure out that he's nothing special." Sandy flopped back in the grass and put her arms behind her head, just like Hec.

81

If Hec had been a rocket, he would have lifted off right then and there. As it was, he didn't need boosters. His heart was already halfway to the moon.

THE END

Like **Tweet Sarts**? Look for other stories
about the Anderson family.
Coming soon.

Every story has to come to an end.
I hope the same isn't true with my
relationship with Charly and Patrice,
without whose help this book would
never have been published.

My eternal gratitude to Matt Bohnhoff.
Son, you have taught me so much
about life and love and art.

TURN THE PAGE TO FIND
OTHER BOOKS FOR MIDDLE GRADE
READERS
WRITTEN BY JENNIFER BOHNHOFF
AVAILABLE
IN PAPERBACK AND EBOOK
AT YOUR FAVORITE ONLINE
BOOKSELLER

Jennifer Bohnhoff

Code: Elephants on
the Moon

And now some special messages," the radio
announcer said. "The siren has bleached hair.
Electricity dates from the twentieth century. The
moon is full of elephants." None of this makes
any sense to Eponine Lambaol, a Breton girl
stranded with her mother in a Norman village on
the coast of France. Nothing has made sense since
the German army moved into France in the spring
of 1940. As rumors of an allied invasion on D-
Day loom ever closer, Eponine joins the
Resistance, where she learns some dark family
secrets that allow her to follow her own
conscience and to understand that the coded
messages on the radio are fraught with more
danger than she could have ever believed
possible.

On Fledgling Wings

Nathaniel Marshal is a bully with a short temper and an empty place in his heart left by the mother who disappeared when he was a baby. The spoiled boy can't wait to leave boring Staywell and begin training so he can become a knight like his father, the cold and distant Sir Amren. But when he arrives at Farleigh, he finds himself in a place of death and danger. Set in the period of Richard the Lionheart, this is a coming of age story about a boy who must confront issues that many modern boys will recognize: the need to control one's temper and destiny, the quest for acceptance, the desire for fitting in, and the awakening of love.

Jennifer Bohnhoff

The Bent Reed
A Novel About
Gettysburg

It's June of 1863 and Sarah McCoombs feels isolated and uncomfortable when her mother pulls her from school and allows a doctor to treat her scoliosis with a cumbersome body cast. She thinks life can't get much worse, but she's wrong.

Physically and socially awkward, 15-year-old Sarah thinks her life is crumbling. She worries about her brother Micah and neighbor Martin, both serving in the Union Army. She frets over rumors that rebel forces are approaching the nearby town of Gettysburg. When the McCoombs farm becomes a battle field and then a hospital, Sarah must reach deep inside herself to find the strength to cope as she nurses wounded soldiers from both sides. Then she must find even more courage to continue to follow her dreams despite her physical disabilities and her disapproving mother.

About the Author

Jennifer Bohnhoff writes novels and teaches middle school social studies in Albuquerque, New Mexico, where she lives with her husband and a petulant cat who does not appreciate her writing in the least.

If you enjoyed reading this book, Jennifer Bohnhoff would love to hear from you.

She'd also be very grateful if you left a review at Amazon, Goodreads, or your favorite site for books for middle grade and young adult readers.

Visit her website at
https://www.jenniferbohnhoff.com

Like her on Facebook at
https://www.facebook.com/
JenniferBohnhoffAuthor

For images related to her stories, check out
https://www.pinterest.com/jbohnhoff/

Made in the USA
Middletown, DE
07 April 2022